SISTER RABBIT'S TRICKS

Emmett "Shkeme" Garcia

Illustrated by

Victoria Pringle

UNIV... | ALBUQUERQUE

© 2013 by Emmett "Shkeme" Garcia

Illustrations © 2013 by Victoria Pringle

All rights reserved. Published 2013

Printed in Singapore by Tien Wah Press Pte Limited

18 17 16 15 14 13   1 2 3 4 5 6

Library of Congress Cataloging-in-Publication Data

Garcia, Emmett Shkeme, 1969–

Sister Rabbit's tricks / Emmett "Shkeme" Garcia ; illustrated by Victoria Pringle.

      p. cm.

ISBN 978-0-8263-5268-2 (pbk. : alk. paper) — ISBN 978-0-8263-5269-9 (electronic)

1. Indians of North America—Folklore. 2. Rabbit (Legendary character)

I. Pringle, Victoria, 1985– ill. II. Title.

E98.F6G28 2013

398.2089'97—dc23

2012017307

DESIGN AND LAYOUT:

Melissa Tandysh

Text is composed in 19/25 ITC Clearface Regular

Display type is Mambo Medium

To

LaDonna Harris,

founder of Americans for Indian Opportunity,

for her global vision,

Pat Melody

of Thunderbird Bird Theater

at Haskell Indian Nations University,

for inspiring creative foundations,

and

Peter Pringle,

for his literary tenacity!

Sister Rabbit enjoyed visiting her friends and relatives in the forest. Most of the time she would have fun . . .

. . . but sometimes Sister Rabbit would play tricks and get into

TROUBLE.

One day, she went to visit Buzzard. Buzzard was very proud of the colorful feathers he had on his head. Sister Rabbit told Buzzard she would teach him how to do the Fire Dance.

"Brother Buzzard, I have many friends who travel a long way just to see me do the Fire Dance," said Sister Rabbit. Buzzard was impressed and wanted to learn the dance.

First, Sister Rabbit made a crown of twigs, leaves, and grass. She put the crown on Buzzard's head and then made a small fire. Sister Rabbit warned, "Don't stop dancing until I am done singing. If you do, something terrible will happen!" She lit the crown on Buzzard's head and began to beat on a hollow log with a stick. Then she began to sing as loudly as she could.

All the animals from around the forest came to see Buzzard dancing the Fire Dance. Soon, the crown of twigs, leaves, and grass began to catch fire, scorching the colorful feathers on Buzzard's head! But Sister Rabbit kept on singing.

Buzzard could not stand the heat any longer. He flew away to the nearest river to dip his head in the water and put out the fire.

Sister Rabbit laughed and laughed and ran away into the forest to find someone else to visit.

Today, Buzzard does not have any more feathers on his head. He's also very shy and embarrassed that his colorful feathers are gone.

The next day, Sister Rabbit came upon Bear, who was fishing in a stream. "Cousin Bear!" Sister Rabbit called. "I know a place where you can have all the honey you can eat!"

Usually, Bear did not like anyone to disturb him while he was fishing, but the taste of honey was better than fish, so he followed Sister Rabbit. Sister Rabbit led Bear to a nearby tree stump.

She told Bear that inside the tree trunk there were tiny Bee Children who liked listening to a good story. If the Bee Children enjoyed the story, they would reward Bear with sweet honey.

Sister Rabbit added,
"When the sun is directly overhead . . .

. . . **Y**ou must remember to take this stick and hit the side of the trunk to let the Bee Children know it is time for lunch."

Bear began to tell the Bee Children about his many adventures, but soon the sun was directly overhead. Bear remembered what Sister Rabbit had told him to do, and so he picked up the stick and hit the side of the trunk.

To Bear's shock, all the Bee Children came swarming out and stung him! Poor Bear ran away, but he was stung so many times he became swollen. Sister Rabbit, who was watching from a distance, laughed and laughed and ran away as fast as she could to find someone else to visit. Today, Bee Children do not trust anyone to visit them. Sometimes, visitors will try to tell them a story, but the Bee Children sting anyone who comes near their nest.

Eventually, Sister Rabbit grew tired of traveling and visiting, so she stopped near a big rock to rest. She made a campfire and sat back to relax. As the fire burned low, turning to ash, Sister Rabbit got bored and began to wonder who to visit next.

*T*hen she spotted Eagle flying high overhead and got an idea. She gathered ashes from the campfire and put them into a hole inside the big rock. Rabbit then waited and waited, and before long, Eagle spotted her and came to visit.

"Uncle Eagle, how good to see you!" Sister Rabbit said. "You look so hungry! I know where you can find something to eat. Just stick your head into that hole, and surely you will find plenty to eat!"

Eagle was very hungry
and happily stuck his
head into the hole.

When Eagle didn't see any food, he pulled his head out of the hole and saw Sister Rabbit laughing at him. Eagle's head was white with ash! Angrily, Eagle turned to Rabbit and said, "Sister Rabbit! You have tricked me and many others for the last time."

"Now **YOU** will be my meal!"

After many days
of being chased,
Sister Rabbit
dug a burrow
underground to
hide in.

Her feet were badly swollen, and she was very sorry for her mean tricks.

Today, Sister Rabbit still enjoys visiting friends and relatives, but she has learned her lesson and does not play tricks anymore.

As a reminder to be good, Sister Rabbit still has big ears, which help her to listen, and big feet, which help her to run away from Buzzard, Bear, and Eagle, who sometimes still chase her around the forest.

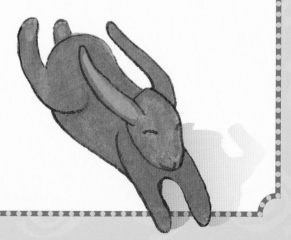